Doc Like Mommy

by **Dr. Crystal Bowe**

Illustrations by
Mike Motz

To my inspirations,
my loves, my children!

Doc Like Mommy

by **Dr. Crystal Bowe**

Illustrations by
Mike Motz

When I grow up,
I know what I want to be...

I want to be a doctor,
just like my mommy!

I'll take care of people,
no matter how small....

Whenever they need me,
I'll answer the call!

I'll tell them what's wrong
if they think they're sick.

I'll make them feel better.
I'll fix them up quick!

I will be there to listen.
I'll be there to care...

Just like my mommy,
I'll always be there!

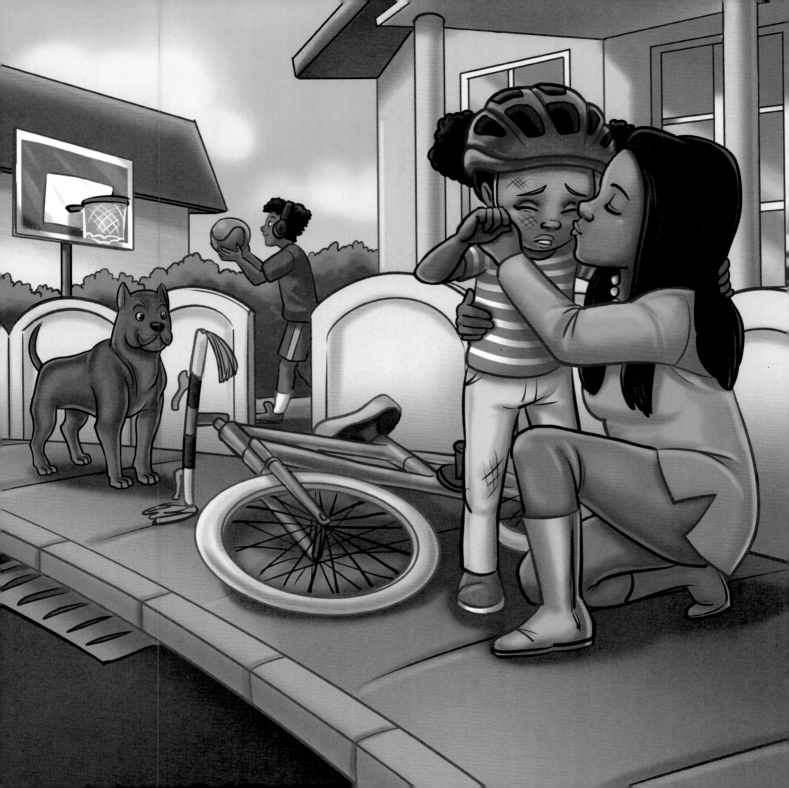

I'll teach people how
they can always stay fit,

I will never stop helping them.
I'll never quit!

One day like my mom,
I may be busy,

But I'll always show my kids,
they're the most important to me!

In the end, no matter
what I grow up to be,

I know my mom will always
be very proud of me!

46665398R00020

Made in the USA
Middletown, DE
06 August 2017